The Unpleasant Tale of
The Man-eating
Christmas Pudding

Leyland Perree   Stuart McGhee

www.glue-publishing.co.uk

First published in Great Britain in 2013 by Ghostly Publishing.
This edition published in Great Britain in 2015 by GLUE kids, an imprint of GLUE Publishing.

The moral right of the author has been asserted.

Visit www.glue-publishing.co.uk for more information.

Connect with the author at www.leylandperree.co.uk
Connect with the illustrator at www.stuartmcghee.com

ISBN: 978-0-9931852-4-3

To Mum, Dad and little sis Gayle
S.M.

To my newest nicest nieces, Honey and Rose
L.P.

And to everyone else...

Merry Christmas!

'Twas the **night** before Christmas...

Its fat little body
Skipped swiftly and nimbly
Up onto the roof
And then with a POOF!
Disappeared down the vicarage chimney.

Covered in soot

It arrived at the foot

Of the stack where a **sock** and two **stockings** hung there.

On the table it spied

A delicious **mince pie**

And some milk.

And it leapt up on top with a cry:

"I'm a Man-eating Christmas Pudding!
Do you not know who I am?
My holly is **prickly**. I'm sticky and sickly.
And covered in Apricot jam!"

MR SANTA

It **scowled** at the pie on the plate and the milk
And it kicked them both over — the mischievous Pud.
Then it **danced** on the crumbs and it **tore** up the note
That the vicarage children had left with the food.

As the pie and the milk sailed over its head
The vicarage kitten **woke up** with a yawn
And, seeing the Pudding, it turned and it fled
And didn't come back 'til the morn.

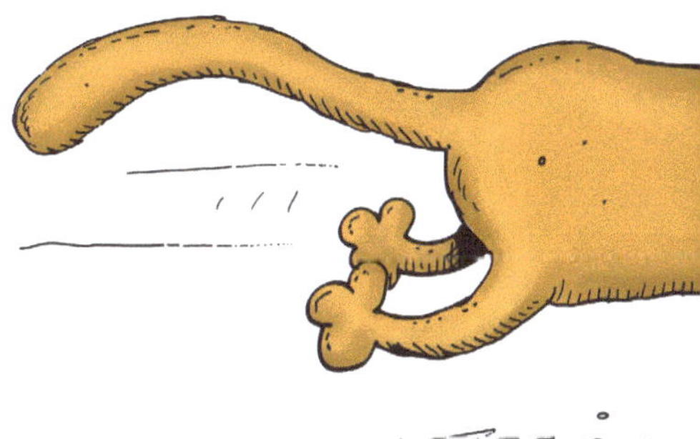

Then the **Man-eating Christmas Pudding**
Ran into the room with the tree
And on all of the **presents**
Did something **unpleasant**
I'd rather you just didn't see.
And **Oh!** How he chortled
While smashing the baubles
And tying the tinsel in knots.
And to make it more **scary**
Dismembered the fairy
To sell her on eBay in lots.

"I'm a **Man-eating Christmas Pudding!**
Do you not know what I do?
I'm evil, malicious, yet **wholly** delicious
And here to **spoil** Christmas for you!"

Still singing his song he leapt up to the mantle
And, grabbing the **cards** and the **notes** of good cheer,
He threw them all into the fire
Then **laughing**
Ran into the hall
With a sneer.

Down came the mistletoe.

Down came the berries.

Down came the portrait of Great Uncle Mary.

Down came the streamers, the angels, the chimes.

And Up went the Pudding three stairs at a time!

WHICH WITCH IS WHICH?

He **messed up** the bedrooms of Johnny and Sue.
He **messed up** the bathroom and **blocked up** the loo.
He **messed up** the nursery, and then he thought **maybe**
He'd toothpaste a **beard** and **moustache** on the baby!
Capering! Naughtiness!
Terrible stuff!
Stickiness! Ickiness!
Feathers and **fluff!**
Stockings in tatters and lanterns in shreds.
And all while the folk lay asleep in their beds.

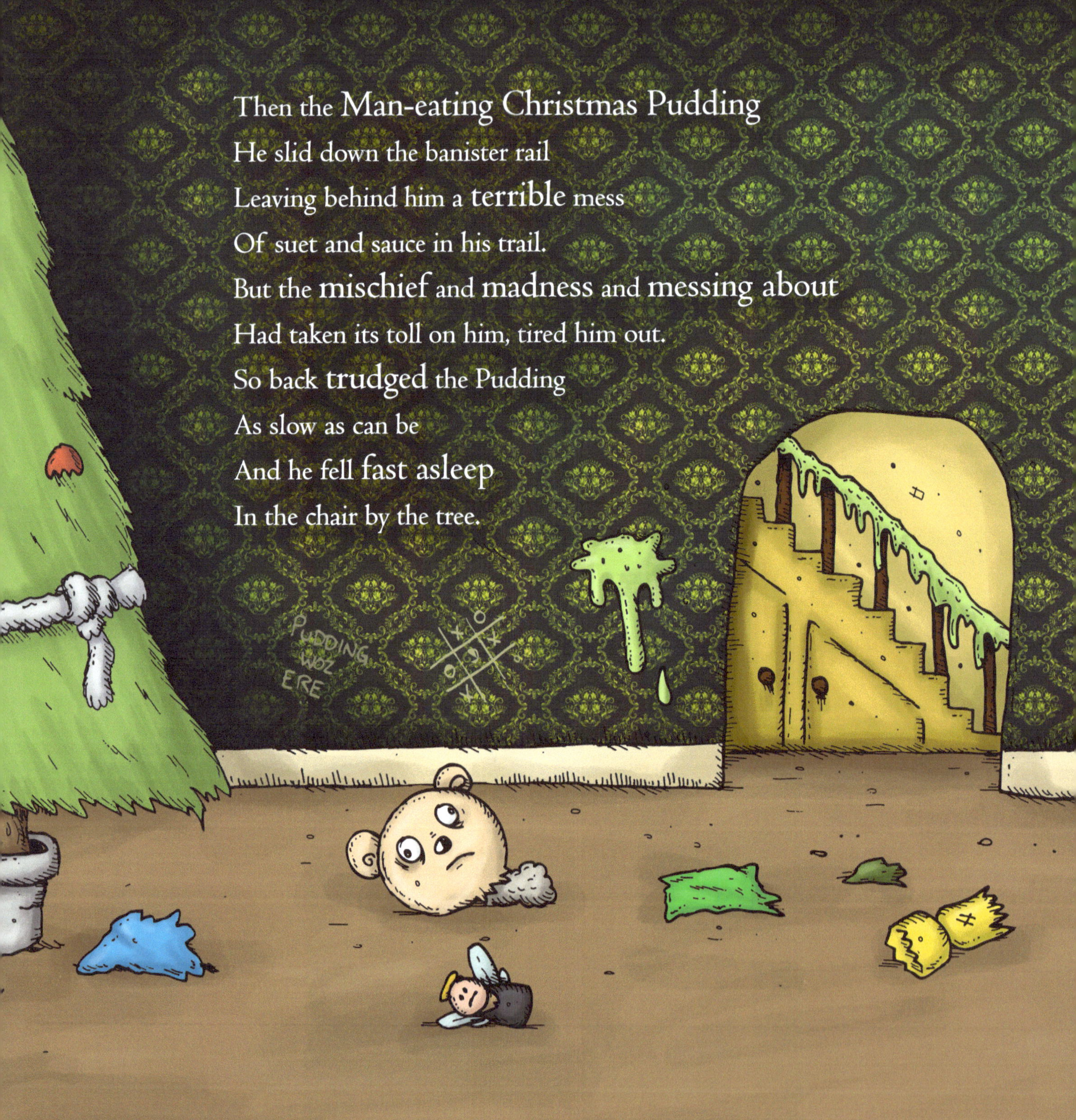

Then the Man-eating Christmas Pudding
He slid down the banister rail
Leaving behind him a **terrible** mess
Of suet and sauce in his trail.
But the **mischief** and **madness** and **messing about**
Had taken its toll on him, tired him out.
So back **trudged** the Pudding
As slow as can be
And he fell **fast asleep**
In the chair by the tree.

Just after **midnight** he woke with a start

And a feeling of dread in his **lack** of a heart.

Just what was that **scuffling, scraping** and tearing?

That **coughing** and **sneezing;** a good deal of **swearing?**

Then out of the stack came a **trickle** of soot.

And a muffled "**ho-ho!**" – and a **boot on a foot!**

And the noise, oh it **grew!**

And it grew!

And it grew!

Until something

popped out of the flue!

From a big cloud of soot stepped a figure in red
With a floppy felt hat on the top of his head
Slung on his back
Was a big bulging sack
And the man looked around as he said:

"Just look at this place! What a terrible mess!
Is there anything, Pudding, you'd like to confess?"

And the Pudding shrank back with a look of distress
Then licking his lips he said:

"Actually, yes…"

"I'm a Man-eating —"

"Enough!"

said the man, and he pulled up a stool.
"Do you take Santa for some kind of fool?
I know who you are, and I know you're not nice.
Do you know how I know?
Well, I checked my list...twice!
Yes, you're on the naughty list, right at the top.
This ruining Christmas — it just has to stop!
You're not a "Man-eater"; that stuff is a lie —

Gah!

Look at my milk
and that ruined mince pie!
That does it!
You're setting it all back to rights.
You'll fix up this place
If it takes you all night!"

So with **trembling** lips
       And a **squeak** like a mouse
The Pudding leapt up
       And ran all 'round the house
Cleaning and tidying,
       Fixing and **glueing**,
Straightening, polishing,
       Mischief-undoing.

He cleaned up the baby.
       He unclogged the loo.
He dusted the mantle (and **Santa Claus** too).
He **rewrote** the notes in his **"bestest"** handwriting.
He rebuilt the fairy to not be so **frightening**.
He rewrapped the presents.
And then, **last** of all
That Great Uncle Mary
Went back on the wall.

Then the **Man-eating Christmas Pudding**
Embarrassed for all that he'd done
Skipped over the rug and gave Santa a hug
And then made for the door at a run.

But Santa said:

"Stop little Pudding!
There's just one more thing to put right."

And he picked up the Pudding

And licking his lips

Proceeded to take

a big bite!

"I'm a Man
eating
Christmas Pudding!"

Roared Santa with gluttonous glee.
He continued to scoff
'Til he'd polished it off...

...and the holly
He hung
On the tree.
JOHN
~ SANTA
SUE
~ SANTA

The End

About the Author

Leyland Perree

Leyland Perree is a freelance children's author.
His children's picture books include *Toad's Road Code*, *The Great Reef Race* and *Which Witch is Which?*

He has worked as a graphic designer, an engineer, a T-shirt printer, a sign-maker,
a customer service advisor for a television company, a page-setter at a local newspaper, in a factory
specialising in handmade industrial rubber goods, and as a typographer within the training industry.

He didn't get the job making authentic replica WWII flight jackets,
which he still thinks would have been pretty darn cool.

Leyland lives with his wife and son in a small village on the edge of Dartmoor,
forty seconds' drive from a zoo.

Visit Leyland's website for further information on works past, present and future:
www.leylandperree.co.uk

If you enjoyed this book by
Leyland Perree and Stuart McGhee
then please rate it on Amazon.
And watch out for other books from this pair of puddings...

★ ★ ★ ★ ★

"A sing-song tale that's a joy
to read out loud"

"Fantastic and thoroughly
recommended"

"Fabulous fun,
perfect for Halloween"

"Quirky and fun"

For further information, visit us at:

www.glue-publishing.co.uk